W9-AVX-562

13 STORIES ABOUT HARRIS

AMY SCHWARTZ

HOLIDAY HOUSE · NEW YORK

For Becky Maroney and Shelly Delaureal

Copyright © 2020 by Amy Schwartz
All Rights Reserved
HOLIDAY HOUSE is registered in the U.S. Patent and Trademark Office.
Printed and bound in March 2020 at Tien Wah Press, Johor Bahru, Johor, Malaysia.
www.holidayhouse.com
First Edition
1 2 3 4 5 6 7 8 9 10

Library of Congress Cataloging-in-Publication data

Names: Schwartz, Amy, author.
Title: 13 stories about Harris / Amy Schwartz.
Other titles: Thirteen stories about Harris
Description: First edition. | New York : Holiday House, [2020] | Audience:
Ages 4–8. | Audience: Grades K–1. | Summary: Thirteen vignettes reveal the everyday life of Harris,
who makes butter with his mother, attends the birthday party of his best friend, Ayana,
and begins preschool in their city neighborhood.
Identifiers: LCCN 2019031155 (print) | LCCN 2019031156 (ebook)
ISBN 9780823442492 (hardcover) | ISBN 9780823443987 (ebook)
Subjects: CYAC: Best friends—Fiction. | Friendship—Fiction.
Neighborhoods—Fiction. | City and town life—Fiction.
Classification: LCC PZ7.S406 Aak 2020 (print) | LCC PZ7.S406 (ebook)
DDC [E]—dc23
LC record available at https://lccn.loc.gov/2019031155
LC ebook record available at https://lccn.loc.gov/2019031156

one

Harris was drawing a dragon on
the sidewalk. It had a very long tail.

It was so
long that it
went around Harris's
tree and past Ayana's house and
around Mrs. Gonzalez and around the corner

and around the fire
hydrant and past the falafel shop
and up and down the No Parking sign
and around the mailbox and back past Mrs. Gonzalez.
The dragon's tail was so long that when he stopped drawing,

Harris was right back
where he'd begun.

two

Harris was standing on his truck
and he shouldn't have been.

three

Harris's mother asked Harris to please open
the refrigerator. She took a little carton of
cream off the middle shelf. She poured
some into a jar.

Harris shook the jar
back and forth and
back and forth and
back and forth.

He shook the jar
up and down and
up and down and
up and down.

Then Harris's mother opened the
jar and there was butter inside.

mmmmm

She spread the butter on toast with
some strawberry jelly and Harris
and his mother ate it for lunch.

four

Harris had never been to a birthday party
before but he was invited to Ayana's.
Harris was wearing his white sweater and
his white shorts and his green shoes.
He looked very nice.

Harris played London Bridge.

And Duck, Duck, Goose.

He ate a piece of chocolate
cake with chocolate frosting
and a scoop of chocolate ice
cream with chocolate sprinkles
and chocolate sauce.

At 3:00 the party was over.
Harris looked very nice.

five

Harris and his mother and father were out for a walk. It was so windy that Harris's mother's shopping list blew right out of her hand.

It was so windy that Harris's hat
blew off of his head and he had to
run and catch it and put it back on.

It was so windy that a big branch fell off of Harris's tree and Harris's father had to call the City to come and pick it up and take it away. It was a very windy day.

six

It was Thanksgiving and Harris was a truck.
He was a truck all the way to his grandmother's house.
He was a truck while he ate turkey and
gravy and mashed potatoes and peas.

He was a truck while he
played checkers with his
grandmother.

And he was a truck when
he took a nice walk outside.

And Harris was a truck all the way home.

seven

Stanley was a hamster. He belonged to
Ayana, and Harris was watching him.

Today was the day to
clean Stanley's cage.
Harris tore a newspaper
into little strips.

Harris's mother refilled
Stanley's water bottle.

She put some hamster
food in Stanley's dish.
"Harris, look!"
Harris's mother said.

Harris looked. There were six tiny
pink baby hamsters next to Stanley.

Harris and his mother were very surprised.

eight

"That's why they call permanent markers permanent,"
Harris's mother said.

ten

Harris and his mother were visiting preschool.
Harris and the preschool lady played blocks.

The preschool lady threw Harris a ball. Harris threw it back.

"Harris," the preschool lady said.

"Can you tell me the names of three different animals?"

"Toucan," Harris said. "Cheetah. Gnu."

"Harris," the preschool lady said, "what do you like to do for fun?"

"I like to put grapes and mashed potatoes on my head," Harris said.

"Harris," the preschool lady said, "is a very interesting child."

eleven

Harris and Ayana were at the beach. Harris took off
his sneakers and his polka-dot socks and Ayana took
off her sneakers and her yellow socks with dinosaurs.

They found some shells and put them in buckets.

They built a castle and dug a very deep hole.

Then Harris and Ayana put their socks and sneakers
back on because it was time to go home.

At bath time Harris took off his sneakers. Then he took off one polka-dot sock and one yellow sock with dinosaurs.

And so did Ayana.

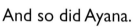

twelve

Harris and Ayana were in preschool.

Harris decided to make a scary mask out of cardboard and construction paper and paper towel tubes and toilet paper tubes.

The mask had scary
teeth and scary eyes,
and Harris wanted to
make a scary nose too.
Harris glued a toilet paper
tube onto his mask.
He wanted to glue
another on top.

"That might not work," Harris's teacher said.

"Yes it will," Harris said.
And it did.

thirteen

Harris and Ayana were holding hands.
They were in the park and they were
going to hold hands forever and ever.

Even if the strongest
man in the world tried
to pull them apart.

Even if they were riding on elephants that were
trumpeting and stampeding and trumpeting.

Even if it was snowing and it kept snowing harder
and harder and their mothers and fathers said,
"Please, please, stop holding hands!"
"Come home right away!"

Harris and Ayana were
going to hold hands
forever and ever.